Briton's Beach Adventures
Dolphins Surprise

Written by: Beth Ann Scullin-Oliphant
Illustrated by: Ashley DelSignore

Dedication

This series is dedicated to all of you beach chair carrying parents and grandparents with hot sandy toes, and of course all of your little sand crabs.

To my husband Joe and children Briton, Amelia, and Judah "Bear" thank you for being my daily inspiration.

Special thanks to my dad, the one who showed me how putting pen to paper can make an impact, and always helped me find my way.

Illustrations by Ashley DelSignore

ISBN: 9798605343295

happyselfpublisher.com

A sleepy Briton arose from bed.
The sun was shining upon his head.

It was a perfect day at the shore.

He was excited to explore.

Mommy helped him to prepare,

swim suit and sunscreen he must wear.

He scurried down
the wooden stairs,
daddy in tow,
a matching pair.

Off to begin his beach adventure.
What memories will little Briton capture?

He shuffled his feet through the sand,

with a shovel and bucket in his hand.

His eyes opened wide as he looked to see

an ocean so endless,
and clear as can be.

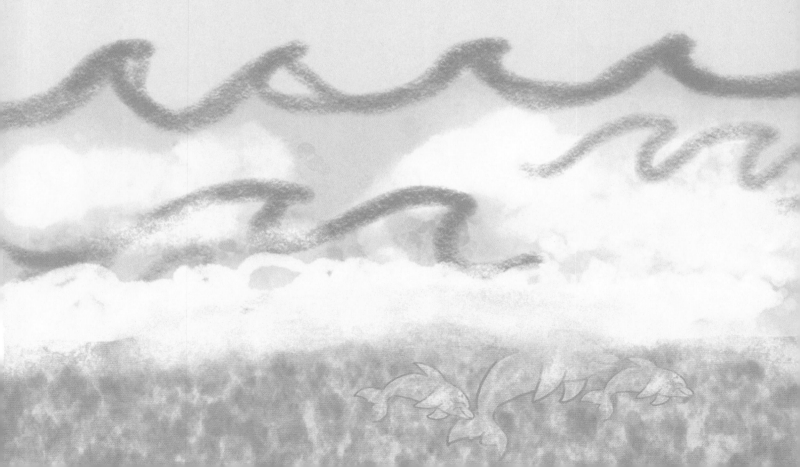

When he reached water's edge,
what did he find?

Five playful dolphins, jumping waves in line!

They soared from the ocean up so high.

A dolphins' surprise!
They could kiss the sky!

As they dove back down they each gave a wink.

Briton was so amazed he could hardly blink!

He ran to his mommy to tell her what he had seen,

aerobatic dolphins of blue, pink and green!

He smiled and waved grinning ear to ear.
A day on the beach was full of cheer!

Play Along with Briton

How many dolphins can you find in the book?

Can you count all of the fishes?

What is your favorite beach activity?

Can you trace the dolphin?

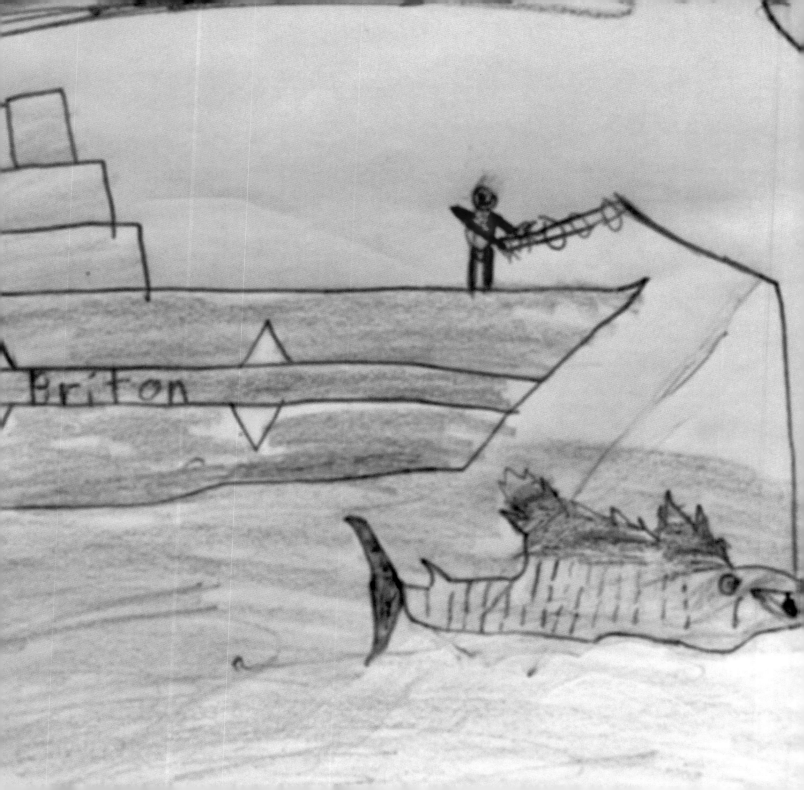

Made in the USA
Monee, IL
09 March 2020